Walt Disney's

AMERICAN CLASSICS

Brer Rabbit in the Briar Patch

Twin Books

MALLARD PRESS

Folks often tell tales of a clever little critter named Brer Rabbit, who lived deep in the woodsy part of the South.

Also in that woodsy part of the South there lived Brer Fox and Brer Bear.

They all called each other Brer, which is short for "Brother."

And they were forever playing tricks on each other.

Now Brer Rabbit had a habit of being plain old rabbity—always a-bouncin' and a-prancin' and acting mighty sassy. He'd always been that way, even way back when he was just a little bunny growing up in the briar patch.

He was rabbity enough to be plain irritating to people. He'd come hoppin' *lippity-clippity* down the road, bold as you please, just like the whole world belonged to him and him alone.

One day Brer Fox and Brer Bear were sittin' around as usual with nothin' better to do than get themselves into some sort of mischief.

As Brer Rabbit came hoppin' past *lippity-clippity,* they were talking about how rabbity and sassy he was.

Brer Fox said "Hold it! I've got a *mighty fine* idea! Hee-hee! Let's go make us a Tar Baby! Brer Rabbit'll get stuck on it, and then we can CATCH him!"

So Brer Fox and Brer Bear rounded up a mess of tar, and patted and rolled and packed it down into a kind of baby shape.

They dressed the Tar Baby in an old hat and a coat. Then they sat it down near the road like it was restin', and just waited around whistlin' and hummin', bidin' their time 'til Brer Rabbit would come, *lippity-clippity*, down the road.

Now Brer Fox and Brer Bear knew how prideful Brer Rabbit was—he HATED folks who didn't return a greetin'! And sure enough, that Brer Rabbit came and stopped right in front of the Tar Baby.

"Howdy!" said Brer Rabbit to the Tar Baby. "I say, Howdy-do!"

The Tar Baby was quiet as a stone. Brer Rabbit said, "What's the matter with you? I said howdy-do! Can't you hear me? If you can't, I can holler louder!"

So he hollered louder: "HOWDY-DO!" But the Tar Baby went right on a-sittin', quiet as a stone.

Brer Rabbit grew mighty mad and said, "If you don't say howdy-do by the time I count three, I'm gonna hit you!"

Brer Fox and Brer Bear just about busted with laughin' as Brer Rabbit counted, "one... two... THREE," and let his fist fly right into that Tar Baby's sticky head!

Brer Rabbit's fist stuck in the tar, and he got even madder. "Let go of my hand!" he said, and hit the Tar Baby with his other fist. That stuck, too.

He hollered and struggled, and still couldn't pull his fists loose.

Brer Rabbit said, "Let go of my fists, or I'll KICK you all the way from here to Timbuktu!"

Sure enough, Brer Rabbit stuck his foot into that old Tar Baby right up to the kneecap! And then he kicked with his other foot! Now, with both hands and feet stuck in that old Tar Baby, Brer Rabbit was in a jam for sure.

Brer Fox and Brer Bear came out of the bushes, a-gigglin' and chucklin' for all they were worth.

Brer Rabbit was so mad he couldn't think straight!

"Listen here, whoever y'all are! If you don't let go I'm a-gonna butt you with my HEAD!"

SPLAT! He butted the Tar Baby so that his head was stuck fast, too.

Pretty soon he was stuck *all over*!

"Howdy-do Brer Rabbit!" Brer Fox said.

"My, oh, my! You are in a terrible bind!" said Brer Bear.

Well, now, it was surely true that Brer Rabbit was as stuck as a rabbity rabbit could be.

"Brer Rabbit," said Brer Fox, "it's not good to be so rabbity—see what kind of mess you got stuck in? Now Brer Bear and I are gonna have to eat rabbit stew for dinner!"

Seeing how he was even more stuck than he had figured, Brer Rabbit sure quieted down then.

While Brer Fox gathered kindling wood for the fire, Brer Bear said, "Before we make rabbit stew, I want to knock Brer Rabbit's block off!" And sure enough, Brer Bear came up with a real scary hunk of wood, big enough to knock *any* block off.

"Wait a little minute," said Brer Fox with a wicked grin. "If we're a-gonna eat him, we ought to *hang* him first."

Now Brer Rabbit got an idea of how he could get free. This made him feel a whole heap better, but he kept *acting* scared… that was part of his plan!

"Sure enough, knock my block clean off an' hang me high as the sky—hang me from a *million* trees! But never, oh *NEVER throw me in that briar patch!*" said Brer Rabbit, the sweat just a-pourin' down his face.

"Hey, maybe we oughta *skin* Brer Rabbit," said Brer Fox with the meanest grin you ever did see.

Brer Rabbit just whooped and hollered, fit to be tied if ever anybody was fit to be tied. "Knock off my block! Hang me! Skin me *up* and skin me *down*, but please, *please*, PLEASE don't you ever throw me into that briar patch!"

"Sounds like he's mighty 'fraid of that stickery old briar patch!" said Brer Bear, still wantin' to knock Brer Rabbit's block off.

Brer Fox gave a nasty giggle. "Maybe we oughta just stick this miserable old rabbit right smack dab in that briar patch! Hee-hee-hee!"

"No! No! Do anything, but PLEASE don't throw me into that terrible ol' briar patch!" yelled Brer Rabbit for all he was worth.

But Brer Bear and Brer Fox went right ahead and threw that poor ol' rabbit right into the biggest, meanest, nastiest mess of brambles you ever did see.

Brer Rabbit shouted "Ow! Oh! Ouch! Ack! Ugh!" and then his shouts just got weaker and weaker. Pretty soon, he wasn't shouting at all, and it was silent in the briar patch.

Brer Fox and Brer Bear laughed, 'cause they figured they'd taken care of pesky ol' Brer Rabbit for good.

Then they heard, "Howdy-do, Brer Fox and Brer Bear!"

It was Brer Rabbit at the other end of the briar patch! The tar had been pulled clean off by the brambles and it lay in a sticky heap deep in the briar patch.

He said, "I *told* you not to throw me in the briar patch! I was *tryin'* to *help* you, but no, sirree! You wouldn't listen. And I fooled you, cause that's the one place y'all will never get me! That's where I was BORN!"

First published in the United States of
America in 1989 by The Mallard Press.

Mallard Press and its accompanying design
and logo are trademarks of
BDD Promotional Book Company, Inc.

Produced by
Twin Books
15 Sherwood Place
Greenwich, CT 06830

ISBN 0-792-45055-8

Designed, edited and illustrated by
American Graphic Systems, San Francisco

Printed in Hong Kong in 1990